DEDICATIONS

I would personally like to thank the people that really helped me to make this story possible. They were my school teachers, the professional educators that taught, guided, persuaded me to be creative. Thank you. To the present and future professional teachers, many mahalo's for your dedication to the world's youth.

— *Ed Freiler*

To my nieces, nephews and second cousins who keep me young at heart.

— *Jeff Pagay*

Published and distributed by

ISLAND HERITAGE
P U B L I S H I N G

99-880 IWAENA STREET, AIEA, HAWAII 96701-3202
PHONE: (808) 487-7299 • Fax: (808) 488-2279
EMAIL: hawaii4u@islandheritage.com

ISBN#: 0-89610-328-5
First Edition, First Printing - 1999

THE KAMA'AINA GECKO II
WHERE'S THE WATER?

Written by **ED FREILER**

Illustrated by **JEFF PAGAY**

ISLAND HERITAGE

Uncle Alakai called out for all the gecko cousins in Ginger Falls.

"Suwanna, Eke, Miki, Owen, everybody in the 'Ohana, please come gather around for a meeting."

Uncle Alakai watched over the cousins in Ginger Falls. When Uncle Alakai called, all the cousins hurried . . . this could be very important.

"Is everybody here?" asked Uncle Alakai.

"Yes, Uncle, except for you-know-who!" said Suwanna.

From the forest they could hear a plea, "Wait for me! Please wait for me!"
It was Owen. He was always late for anything and everything, except time to eat.

After Owen scooted to a stop, Uncle Alakai said, "Mahalo to all of you for showing up at this meeting. I have some very important news about our precious swimming hole."

Uncle Alakai looked very serious, so all the cousins moved in real close to listen.

"The water in the swimming hole is getting very low," Uncle Alakai explained. "The waterfall has hardly any water flowing over it."

"I cannot even go underwater. It's too shallow!" said Eke, the Kamaʻaina Gecko.

5

"**I**s water important, Uncle?" asked Owen.

"Very important, Owen. Very important indeed," said Uncle Alakai.

"All the plants and trees need water to grow, don't they, Uncle Alakai?" asked Suwanna.

"Yes they do, Suwanna," stated Uncle Alakai. "Everything needs water — it helps us grow and keeps us clean and healthy."

"This is not good. I want to be clean and healthy," said Miki.

All the other cousins yelled out, "We want to be healthy too!"
"What can we do?" asked Miki.
"What can we do too?" asked all the cousins.

7

"Something is wrong far up the valley," said Uncle Alakai. "The stream may be blocked with something."

"I will go and look to see what is wrong," said Eke.

"I will go with him," said Suwanna.

"I will go too!" said Owen.

"We will all go!" yelled the cousins.

"Good for all of you," smiled Uncle Alakai. "The trip will be a long one, lasting overnight."

8

"Overnight! Away from Ginger Falls!" gasped Miki.

None of the cousins had ever been away from Ginger Falls overnight.

"What about the *holoholona*?" yelled Owen.

Almost every night, deep within the forest, strange noises were heard . . . grunting, snorting, and wild footsteps tearing through the forest. It was very loud and scary. All the young cousins believed it was the *holoholona*, a wild beast.

"Yes, something does live out there, but you will be okay. Do not be afraid of a noise in the dark. It could be a friend," said Uncle Alakai.

"I — I will go anyway," gulped Eke. But even when he said he would go, he was staring into the forest.

"I will go too," said Suwanna. "We need the water very much."

Nobody else said a word. All the cousins moved a little closer to Uncle Alakai. They really did not want to be away from Ginger Falls overnight. All of them were thinking about the *holoholona*.

Owen stepped away, "Um, I, Um, I can help save the water here at Ginger Falls. Yes, I will make sure we don't waste any water," said Owen.

"We don't want to waste any water either," said all the cousins.

Uncle Alakai knew Eke and Suwanna would be safe and he knew that the others cousins were a little frightened.

"I think that is a fine idea," said Uncle Alakai. "Suwanna and Eke will go, and the rest of you can help conserve the water here. Both jobs are very important."

"We must always conserve water in Hawai'i," said Suwanna. "And we can do our part right here at Ginger Falls."

All the cousins started to do things to conserve water.

12

Later that day, Eke and Suwanna got ready to leave Ginger Falls.

"Aloha, Cousins," said Suwanna. "We are leaving now."

"Aloha," said Uncle Alakai waving good-bye.

"Be careful!" said Miki.

"Be careful!" yelled all the cousins.

13

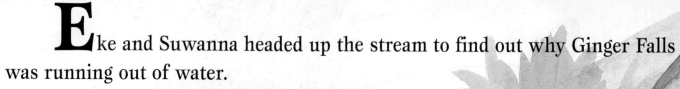

Eke and Suwanna headed up the stream to find out why Ginger Falls was running out of water.

"Uncle, what will they eat?" asked Owen.

"Owen, I knew you would ask that," laughed Uncle Alakai. "They will eat bugs and fish, the same as they do here!"

14

Eke and Suwanna had traveled very far following the almost empty stream. The sun had started to set and looked beautiful against the mountains surrounding the forest. Suwanna loved to look at the sky during sunset.

"Eke, isn't this the most beautiful time of the day?" asked Suwanna.

"Yes, it is, Suwanna — but you would say the same thing in the morning when the sun rises," laughed Eke. "Suwanna, you love everything!"

"You are right, Eke. I do love everything, except mud!" stated Suwanna.

"We need to stop and find a place to sleep," said Eke. "It will be dark soon."

Eke found a big tree to sleep under and Suwanna climbed onto a branch, just above Eke. Both were very tired and fell asleep right away. Everything was nice and peaceful.

CRASH! SNORT! SCRAPE! SCRAPE! GRUNT!
Loud noises from the dark forest startled Eke and Suwanna.
"Eke, it's the *holoholona*!" whispered Suwanna in a shaky voice.

The noises got closer and closer — and louder and louder. This frightened Eke and Suwanna and they huddled close.

Then the noises went away! It was nice and peaceful just like before. Eke and Suwanna soon fell right back to sleep.

The rising sun that morning was as beautiful as ever. Eke and Suwanna woke up and continued on their journey to find the reason for the water shortage.

"Were you afraid last night?" Suwanna asked Eke.

"A little bit, but I remembered that Uncle Alakai said noises could be our friends and not to be afraid," answered Eke.

"I was afraid a little bit too, but I knew that you were here, and having someone with you helps you not to be afraid," said Suwanna.

They walked along the top of a hill above the stream. All of a sudden Eke tripped on the grass and started to slide down a muddy trail. Suwanna was riding on his back and could do nothing but hold on.

"AY-YI-YI-YI!" screamed Suwanna.

"WHEEEEE!" yelled Eke as the two of them slid toward a big, giant, gooey mud puddle.

KA-PLUEY! KA-PLOP!

Eke and Suwanna landed in the mud. Both of them were covered from head to toe with the gooey, sticky, yucky mud.

"OOH! I don't like the mud!" exclaimed Suwanna.

"**A**re you okay, Suwanna?" asked Eke.

"Okay? You ask me if I'm okay! I'm covered all over with gooey, sticky, yucky mud!" screamed Suwanna.

From the other side of the mud puddle, a deep voice asked, "What's wrong with the mud?"

"Who said that?" asked a surprised Suwanna.

"It wasn't me," said Eke.

"It was *me!*" said the deep voice again.

Suwanna pointed to a large muddy blob with two big eyes and two large teeth. It looked like the mud puddle was alive!

25

"IT'S THE *HOLOHOLONA!*" screamed Suwanna.
Eke could not believe his eyes and couldn't say a word.
"I'm not a *holoholona*, I'm a wild pig!" said the blob. He shook
wildly and the mud came off. Sure enough, it was a wild pig!

"**A**loha, my name is Hulos," said the wild pig.

Eke and Suwanna could not find their voices.

Then Eke said, "Aloha, I'm Eke. I'm the Kama'aina Gecko."

"I'm Suwanna. I'm sorry I called you a *holoholona*. But I thought you were the *holoholona* that ran through the forest at night," said Suwanna.

Hulos laughed, "That was me you heard last night! I eat roots and berries and look for them at night when it is cool. Then during the daytime while it is hot, I rest in cool places like this mud puddle."

Eke and Suwanna laughed very hard.

"What is so funny?" asked Hulos.

"Last night we were so scared when we heard you," said Suwanna. "I can't wait to tell our cousins in the 'Ohana at Ginger Falls that we met the *holoholona* and he is very nice."

"Why are you so far from home?" asked Hulos.

"We are running out of water at Ginger Falls and are looking for the reason why," said Eke.

"I think I know the reason why you don't have water flowing downstream," said Hulos. "Follow me!"

So off went Eke, Suwanna, and their new friend to see what the problem was.

29

Hulos took them to a place upstream where there was a big pile of rubbish right in the middle of the stream. The rubbish had formed a dam blocking the water. There was an old slipper with a broken strap, old cans, empty bottles, plastic bags, even a broken beach chair. All of this stuff was blocking the stream, preventing the water from flowing downstream to Ginger Falls.

"This is awful!" said Suwanna. "What is this stuff?"

"It is called rubbish," said Hulos. "Rubbish is something that no one wants any more. It ends up here in our beautiful forest if it is not disposed of properly."

"What can we do about this?" asked Eke.

"I know!" exclaimed Suwanna. "Eke, you can push it out of the way with your tail!"

"Great idea," said Hulos. "And I can help — I can push it with my snout!"

Suwanna climbed up a tree to watch as both Eke and Hulos started to work to clear the rubbish from the stream.

They did a wonderful job, and Suwanna yelled and clapped.
The water started flowing down the stream just like before!
"This is so wonderful!" yelled Suwanna excitedly. "Mahalo to both of you."

"Mahalo to you, Hulos," said Eke. "Now we must get back to Ginger Falls."

"It was nice to meet both of you and I hope we meet again. Aloha, my friends." said Hulos.

"Aloha, Hulos." said Suwanna and Eke together.

Back at Ginger Falls, the cousins watched as the water flowed over the falls, just like always. But they learned that water is very precious and we must always conserve how we use it, even when we have plenty.

Eke and Suwanna told about their trip and meeting Hulos (instead of a *holoholona*) and the rubbish dam, and everything else.

Uncle Alakai just watched the young geckos and smiled. Why? Because that is what old wise ones do when young ones learn.

KE HOPENA (THE END).